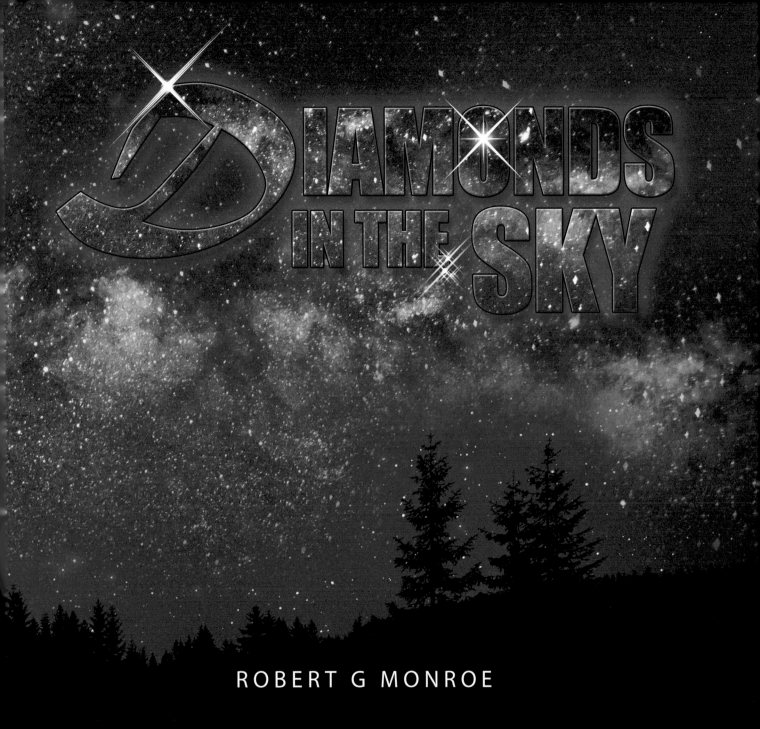

DIAMONDS IN THE SKY

ROBERT G MONROE

ISBN: Softcover   978-1-9845-2605-2
         EBook   978-1-9845-2604-5

Print information available on the last page

Rev. date: 05/07/2018

To order additional copies of this book, contact:
Xlibris
1-888-795-4274
www.Xlibris.com
Orders@Xlibris.com

Barbara was tired. She had been going all day, and she felt drained. Ever since she had decided to stay at NASA and devote herself to the project, work was just about all she had been doing. The work was important, she knew that, but neglecting her social life was not a good choice to make. She checked the meal that was slow cooking in the Crock-Pot. It was done. She made a plate for herself and sat down to eat. Beef stew was one of her favourite dishes. She often ate it without rice though. That was to conserve calories.

It worked too. Her figure was absolutely lovely, which was a remarkable thing considering that she was the mother of four children. They were all grown. One actually worked with her on the project. After finishing her meal, Barbara set her dishes in the sink. She carefully washed them then dried them. She put them away easily. Then she drew herself a hot bath.

Barbara slowly lowered herself into the hot bath. She found such things incredibly relaxing. She let the day's cares fall away. She knew that she would sleep well tonight. She decided that she would let tomorrow's cares and concerns be for tomorrow. Tonight, she would just relax. Tomorrow was Friday. If she so desired, she could take half the day off, and she and her children could spend some quality time together.

Yes, Barbara thought as she methodically dried off. She would send out invitations for her four children to join her this weekend. They had all been working hard themselves. Also, she was concerned as to just when they would get around to making her a grandmother. It would be at little short notice, but she felt they would be able to attend. Her little gatherings were always informal.

They were also beneficial, in Barbara's considered opinion. They offered her family, her immediate family, the opportunity to be a sounding board for themselves. They could often produce great ideas by combining and comparing and contrasting their thoughts.

Barbara turned on the TV and lay down on her bed to watch. A little TV would help her to relax, and then she would go to sleep. She looked at the TV screen and saw the Congress debating the budget. After watching for fifteen minutes, it became clear that they were not proposing cutting NASA's budget. Barbara relaxed and went to sleep.

Barbara was dreaming she was on Mars. She and the rest of the team were doing work necessary to prepare Mars for permanent human habitation. Neal, who was a very close friend of Barbara's, had the job of testing the soil to make it suitable for Earth microorganisms. Others studied the Martian world for clues as to why it did not have a magnetic field covering the entire world. That question was key, because a continuous magnetic field protected a planet's atmosphere from the solar wind.

They were explorers. They were adventurers. Their mission was to spread life beyond Earth. It would be slow going at first. As they learned, however, their pace would accelerate. Barbara noticed that she was running low on oxygen. She started back for the supply craft and suddenly realized she was dreaming. The dream had been that real. She had thought it was really happening. Now it was fading away. Barbara slept the night away.

Barbara slowly came back to life the next morning. She had really been sleeping hard. She checked her clock that sat on her nightstand. Its digital display read five minutes after eight. Wow, she thought to herself as she arose. She had really overslept. Her days usually started at half past six in the morning. Now she was over an hour and a half late. It was really indicative of just how much she had been overworking herself. She began to dress and thought of her children. She would email them just as soon as she finished dressing herself. It was a fortunate fact that she was not due at the lab until nine o'clock. It meant she might still be on time.

She finished dressing and picked up her phone. Activating the email app, she typed in one of her children's addresses. Then she made carbon copies for the other three. She typed the body of her message, inviting all of them to a cookout at her house that weekend. Then, after she reached into the freezer and placed a microwavable breakfast into the microwave, she called the lab. Then, after advising them that she might be a few minutes late, she had an impromptu discussion on what they would be doing that day. Finally, after finding out that the entire lab had decided to take a half-day off, she said goodbye and hung up the phone.

The microwave beeped out its message that her breakfast was ready. She took it out and sat down to eat. She ate quickly but still enjoyed her breakfast. Then, after quickly brushing her teeth, she was out the door.

Her commute from Bay Saint Louis, Mississippi, to the Stennis Space Center lasted less than fifteen minutes. So instead of being a few minutes late, she actually arrived there fifteen minutes early. The problem at the moment was to calculate the moment of inertia of several key components. Barbara got to work. When her break arrived, she sent emails to all her children except the one who worked with her. While her girls might not show, he was sure to come. Then it was back to work. Several of her problems required extensive computation. However, computer time was precious.

When her turn at the computer had finally come, she was ready. The supercomputer they had been allocated was one of the newest models. It was a one-terraflop machine. That meant that it could perform one trillion calculations per second. Barbara often used the Cray supercomputer to perform something known as numerical integration. It was one of those problems for which computers were perfectly suited. Even with all the computing power at her disposal, it would take about a half hour to perform the computations.

Then it was time for a design meeting. All the various disciplines would attend. They would discuss the design they were working on.

The meeting went well. They would have a workable design by the completion date. Then they could build a prototype and begin actual testing. After the meeting was over, they went back to their respective stations. Barbara's answer had been calculated, she was told. Then it was time for lunch. They all left for the day.

Barbara texted her son. In her message, she asked him if he could meet her at his house. He replied almost immediately, saying that he was going there anyway and he certainly could meet her there. She went by the grocery store to get some things for supper. Then she went to her son's house. It was an uneventful drive, which was a good thing. Her son lived even closer to the jobsite than she did, so it was easy to get there. When she arrived, he was waiting for her on the front porch.

"How was your day?" he inquired as she walked towards him, carrying bags of groceries.

"Fair to middling," she replied as he took some of the bags from her. "We have just about all of the theory worked out. Now we just need a working prototype."

He replied, "We will have that for you soon enough."

"Okay," she replied as they walked inside. "You just get to work right on it."

"Sure," he replied. "First things first though. Let's get started on supper."

"Okay with me," she replied.

They began cooking. Forty-five minutes later, it was almost done. Barbara began sending out text messages to her other children. While she awaited an answer from them, it became time to eat. She sat down at the table with her son. They both had a magnificent bowl of salad before them, along with an even more magnificent plate of spaghetti.

Barbara reached for the Parmesan cheese. She began sprinkling it liberally on her spaghetti. At the same time, her son reached for the salad dressing. He screwed off the cap and began to pour a small amount on his salad. Then they began to eat. "So, do you think that the others will be able to be at your place tomorrow?"

"I believe so," she replied.

Barbara and her son ate in silence. The spaghetti and salad were delicious. After a few moments of silence, her phone began to chime. It was a text from her girls. They would be able to attend her little get-together tomorrow. She sent a reply and spoke to her son.

"We should all have a great time tomorrow," she declared confidently.

"We sure should," her son replied. "I'll sure enjoy seeing all of my sisters." He smiled coyly. "I'll be able to inquire about their love lives."

"You take your life into your own hands making such inquiries," Barbara said humorously.

"Maybe," he replied easily. "However, I believe in the family, as Father and yourself raised me to. Furthermore, I believe that my sisters have been playing the field for far too long. They should really try to find someone special, and I fully realize that that can take quite a long time. But they never will if they never begin really trying."

"Well," she replied, "maybe they are, and we simply aren't aware of it yet. After all, we spend a fair amount of our time apart. I've always thought it is an awful shame that we communicate so little in this day of instant communication. We really should catch up with each other's lives this weekend, and we should *stay* in touch from here on out!"

"I certainly agree with all that you have said." Her son was very easy to get along with. She was proud of the way he handled both himself and his life. He avoided or otherwise handled the anger of others without using violence. He would only use deadly force as a last resort to save himself or his family. "Though as you know, I always prefer persuasion to coercion," he said with just a touch of irony.

"Yes, I know that," she replied. "I was just concerned about my children. Because, as you know, children *never* grow up to their mothers."

"Yes, of course," he replied. "Just let us be gentle with our suggestions."

"Sounds like a plan," she replied. They finished the rest of the meal in silence.

Barbara's son began to speak slowly. "We should begin planning for tomorrow. We really need a game plan for how we are going to approach the girls. I mean, we are really about to go to Mars. The whole of the human race is on the verge of colonizing another planet. We really should get our priorities straight as a family."

"I know," Barbara replied slowly. "Dear Lord, do I know. Except that we must be very careful how we approach them. One wrong word and so much damage could be done."

"Yes," her son replied. "I well know the subtle nature of human communication. True communication, anyway. All three of them—Tasha, Erin, and Tamar— need to be treated very delicately. They need to understand both that we love and support them and that we expect certain conducts out of them. We truly need to understand their needs and wants while also making our position fully understood."

"Just remember," Barbara replied, "that you can lead a horse to water, but you can't make him drink. All we may do is encourage. We cannot command."

"With the right approach, we shouldn't have to command," her son replied. "We should be able to convince them of the need to cooperate."

"We'll see then," Barbara replied. She began to get up, but her son rose first.

"I'll get the dishes," he said easily.

"Okay," Barbara said just as easily. She lowered herself back into the chair. Her son began to clear the table. He began to prepare some water to wash them in. He silently began to wash the dishes. After twenty minutes, the dishes were drying in the dish holder, clean as a whistle.

"Well," said Barbara, "let us, you and I, retire to the living room. We will wait for your siblings there."

"Okay," her son replied easily. "Let's do that."

They went to the living room together. They sat opposite each other in two comfortable recliner chairs. There was the sound of car tires in the driveway outside.

"Well," her son replied easily, "they're here."

"Yes, let us, you and I, begin," Barbara said in earnest. Her son went to the front door and opened it. Barbara's son, Theodore, greeted his wife. They met at the door.

"Hello, Heather," he said easily.

"Hi, Theo," she replied just as easily.

"We're going to have my mother and sisters over tomorrow. Don't worry though. I will do all of the cooking for you."

"Okay," Heather replied easily. "Just help me get some food out of the car please."

"Sure thing," Theodore replied. He walked out of the front door.

They were alone, the man and his wife. "Theodore," she said with a strained voice, "when will we visit my parents again?"

"Whenever they choose to visit us," he replied cautiously.

"When will *we* go to visit them though?" she said vigorously.

"Well, we had planned to go to Bermuda when my part of the project is completed." He chose his words with the utmost discretion. "We could just as easily change our plans and go to the Delta."

"Okay," she said slowly. Heather didn't sound mollified. "Could we stay a long time?" she said impatiently.

"Yes, of course. When my part in the project is finished, when my work is done, *we* will have quite a bit of free time."

"Okay, okay, sheesh, don't yell at me."

Theodore stopped and gazed at his wife. She was beautiful in his eyes. She wore her ebony hair long, but she didn't braid it like some women did. She didn't put it in ponytails or anything like that. She had no curls. She wore it long and straight, and her eyes of ebony matched her hair colour. Heather Rowe was beautiful—in her eyes as well as her husband's.

"Heather, you know I never raise my voice at you. Isn't that why you married me? Because I wasn't just like all the other boys? Because I was gentle?"

His wife gazed at him peevishly. "Yes, I remember," Heather said sardonically. "You are a gentleman."

"Yes," Theodore said gently. "Also, a gentle man."

"That you certainly are." Her smile returned like the sun peeking out from behind the clouds.

She really did love him. Theo was very kind, and her father had certainly approved of him. She just wanted what she wanted. It was as simple as that. Heather thought carefully. If she could get her husband away from work and his *mother*, she and he could have some quality time together. She was ready to have their first child. She had always said she wanted a man, but she was just being coy. What she *really* had wanted was to stay a child forever. She had been raised very permissively by her father. He had really been lax in giving her direction. She had therefore begun to think of life as a show with herself as the star, so she was on the verge of becoming a maiden forever. Theodore had come along and saved her from a fate literally worse than death. She loved him so much, but there was always that little streak of defiance in her.

"Well then, *gentle* man, I would really like to see my daddy."

"Sure," Theodore answered easily. "We can spend a month up there." They took the bags of food inside the house.

Barbara greeted them with a smile. "I hope you two lovebirds are ready for some fun tomorrow."

"We certainly *are*," Heather said with a radiant smile.

"Have you eaten yet?" Barbara asked her daughter-in-law.

"No, not yet," Heather replied. "Don't worry though. I'll have the leftovers."

They smiled pleasantly at each other. The relationships between mothers and their daughters-in-law have been many and varied through the years. Some young men's mothers absolutely *never* want to grow up or see their *sons* grow up. Heather broke eye contact with her mother-in-law. She went to the fridge and began to make selections for her supper. She selected some chicken rotel to eat. She took the bowl out of the refrigerator and put it into the microwave. She selected 75 percent power and set the timer for fifteen minutes.

"Welladay," Heather said reluctantly. "Barbara, what does vacation mean to you?"

"Well, it means that you really need an extended rest," Barbara said uneasily. She knew that Heather could be volatile.

"Exactly!" Heather said excitedly. "Theodore said we would take a long one once his part of the project was finished."

"I have absolutely no problem with that," Barbara said easily.

"Good!" Heather exclaimed excitedly. "It's settled then."

"Yes, I suppose it is," Barbara said slowly.

Heather began to alternately take old food out of and put new food into the refrigerator. She began to put a big bowl into the microwave. She punched ten minutes into the timer and pushed Start. The microwave began to hum. The timer counted down to zero. Heather withdrew her bowl of fettuccine from the microwave oven. She removed the aluminium cover, and the steam issued forth. Heather set the steaming bowl on the island in the middle of the kitchen. Slowly the steam subsided. She opened the cabinet and slowly withdrew a ceramic dinner plate. "Now that we are all in agreement, don't we make a good family?"

Heather ate in silence for an hour and forty-five minutes. Barbara had gone home, and her husband sat opposite her, smiling gently. "You know that you are important to me, Heather."

Heather smiled shyly. "I guess," she said reluctantly.

Theodore said very earnestly, "Well then, let me say it again, Heather. You are beautiful to me."

Heather Rowe Maclaurin smiled radiantly. She had been really happy, since Theodore, with all his efforts, had managed to convince her that he really did love her. Also, that had taken some effort, as Theo could attest to. When he had first spoken to her, on the first day they met no less, she had seemed radiant. Later, as they became friends, she seemed to become distant. It had dawned on him that she might be actually afraid of marriage. It turned out to be literally true. As they became better friends, he asked to meet her parents. That had been the saving grace, Theodore decided later. Theodore believed with all his heart that the fact, the mere fact, that her daddy had received him well and approved of their friendship led her to be friends with him. They were already *friendly towards each other*. However, only her father's approval could have encouraged her to be a true friend to Theo. Of that, he was sure.

"Well," Theo said with confidence, "let me do the dishes, and then we may tell each other about our respective days."

"Aww," Heather said petulantly. "Let the dishes alone till tomorrow, and then we may cuddle on the couch."

Theodore Maclaurin couldn't argue with that.

The next day was Saturday, the day of rest. This was just what Theodore felt lying on the couch—rested. His wife was gone, and then he heard her busy in the kitchen.

"Whoa, man, it lives!" she exclaimed when she heard, then saw, him up and moving around. "I already washed last night's dishes," Heather said sardonically. "Want to take a shower and change, sleepyhead?" she gently chided.

"Uh, sure I will," Theo said quietly. "First of all, though, what's for breakfast?"

"Scrambled eggs for toi, pancakes for moi, and turkey bacon and orange juice for the both of us," Heather said easily.

"Sounds good," Theo replied.

She picked up two plates from the island and began to prepare each of them a plate of food.

Heather sat the two plates on the island. She reached for the two glasses that she had set out. Opening the orange juice jug, she poured two glasses for them. After setting the jug on the island, they began to eat in silence. After a few bites, Heather said vibrantly, "I am really looking forward to our visit to your mother's house. I'm looking forward to speaking with your sisters."

"Yes, so am I," Theodore replied. "Look, Heather, you know I've been thinking. What do you think about us starting a family of our own?"

Heather looked up at her husband in awe and wonder. "Well," she said slowly, "you know that we both want a family." Her face bore that look of wonder that he had been so fascinated by when they had met. She looked as though all of time were held in her eyes. They seemed to take in light yet shine inside of themselves.

"Yes, I do," Theodore responded. "Is now the right time to start a family?"

"It just might be . . ." Her voice trailed off into silence. Her ebony eyes were full of stars. "Well, we can speak of it today. We can speak of it at the family reunion." Her ebony eyes were full of mirth.

"Good. Oh, and by the way, I'm sorry we didn't have time to invite your parents," Theo said regretfully.

"Oh, that's okay, honey. There will be other opportunities for them and us," she replied shyly.

"Sure, there will be," Theodore said slowly.

They continued to eat in silence. Their breakfast was delicious. "This really is good," Theo commented as they ate.

"Thank you," Heather said radiantly.

"Let me get the dishes," Theo said.

"Surely," Heather responded.

Heather glanced at the digital clock on the microwave. It read eight thirty. They were to be at her mother-in-law's house by eleven o'clock. They were way ahead of schedule. "I tell you what. Why don't we spend some quality time together before we go to your mother's house?"

"I believe that is a perfect idea," Theo replied. So they lay down together on the couch and began to plan for new arrivals.

The clock on the wall read ten o'clock. Barbara Maclaurin was busy in her kitchen. A huge bowl of green leafy vegetables was on the island. She had broccoli soup cooking slowly on the stovetop. She stirred the broccoli soup absent-mindedly. It simmered on the stove. The cream was a bright white colour. The slow roiling of the cream gave an elegant appearance to the mixture that sat cooking slowly on the stove. Barbara moved out of the kitchen and into the living room to set the table. The place ware was already there, waiting patiently for her. She began to set her table. She was soon through. The setting was easy. The clear-away was not.

Her guests began to arrive. Barbara was the hostess tonight. Tonight, they would all shine on. Her girls began to walk through the door one at a time. They greeted her one by one. Erin was the first. With her eyes of ebony and her hair of gold, she was beautiful to behold. She walked through to her waiting family. Tasha was the second. With her eyes of green and her red hair all sheen, she walked into the room. Tamar was the third. With her dark skin, her face was polished and cool.

Lastly, Theodore, with his wife, entered the room. Heather surveyed the room and liked what she saw. It was so fun here! This family was so colourful! It was lovely. She really liked raising her cousins, but this was even better. She was glad that she had said yes to Theo.

"Well," Barbara said expansively, "let's talk! Erin, Tasha, Tamar. Please come see me."

The girls stopped and began to pay closer attention. They walked slowly over and stood by their mother. They stared at her intently. They were really interested in what she had to say.

"Girls, this is a momentous occasion for your brother and I. We are just about finished with our part of advancing human progress. The National Aeronautics and Space Agency is, in just under two years, going to launch the first human mission to another planet. We will explore another world in preparation for colonizing it. So I would like us to discuss this family's future."

A sly look overcame Tamar's face. "Oh, I know what this is about," she said slyly. "When are we going to marry?"

"Yes, and to whom?" Barbara said knowingly. "Look, we need to get some things straightened out here. I know you have all enjoyed being free spirits, but really, it's time to come in from the cold. So just *when* are you going to marry?"

The girls looked at their mother incredulously. She had never been so blunt.

"I would like to know that my family will remain healthy when my time here is done. I need to know that your father's legacy will live on in your children. Now, seriously, just when will you get serious with your lives?"

"Oh, okay, Mom," they all said in unison. "We will."

"We're not averse to this. We all even have people in mind. It's a momentous decision. Really, though, we're all just about to get serious with this. We all have men in our lives that we would like to introduce to you. We will next Monday if you can spare a day off from work." Barbara's daughters said together.

"Well," Theo said with a broad grin on his face. "This is really special. We will be able to meet here then."

"Then it's settled. It's about time. I'll leave you ladies and gentlemen to speak among yourselves. Let me step outside and catch my breath," Barbara said with glee. She went to the back door and stepped outside onto her porch. She glanced up at the stars.

Barbara Maclaurin stared at the first stars of the night sky. In just under two years, the first interplanetary spacecraft would take off from the Kennedy Space Center towards Mars.

They could and would go, she knew. With each step completed, they would be ready to take another.

Printed in the United States
By Bookmasters